MW01169491

SPACE STATION

ALSO BY K.R. GADEKEN

THE NABUKKO TRILOGY

Nabukko

Daedalus

NOVELLAS

Space Station

SHORT STORIES

Lakes of Cinnamon

Mr. Safransino

Space Station

A Novella

K.R. Gadeken

Names: Gadeken, K.R., author.

Title: Space Station / K.R. Gadeken.

Identifiers: ISBN 979-8-9904213-3-2 (paperback) | ISBN 979-8-9904213-4-9 (ebook)

Subjects | FICTION / Science Fiction / General | FICTION / Visionary & Metaphysical | FICTION / Absurdist

First Edition: January 2025

Printed in the United States of America

For Allison, Lisa, Cara, Philip, and Jacob

CONTENTS

SPACE STATION

A
NOVELLA

K.R. GADEKEN

PROLOGUE

I stood behind a view panel, staring breathlessly at the colossal system of interconnected spheres on the other side of the glass barrier. My palms were sweaty, my heart thrummed uncomfortably, and I fought the urge to shift my stance every twelve seconds.

There it is. Everything I've been waiting for.

My mouth was dry and hanging open. The light of the type-G star glistened off the white hulls of the spheres, and I sighed wistfully at the site. A faint metallic groan sifted through the walls, but I paid no attention to it.

It's almost time.

A door *whooshed* open behind me, dragging a faint sterile breeze into the room. A garbled, waterlogged voice tried to say something to me, but I ignored it in favor of soaking up a few more moments of staring out at the spheres.

Here I go.

CHAPTER ONE

GARDEN SNAKES

The sun never fully rose and it never fully set, perpetual morning painting the round sky. I was hardly ever tired and almost always cheery. People wandered around in bright clothes, stopping randomly to stack blocks or share snacks or paint the grass purple and blue. The trees smiled at me, the beetles chuckled at my jokes, and the grasshoppers always wanted to see whatever I brought to show them. The birds gave me hugs whenever I wanted, the foxes cuddled next to me on the rare occasions I felt the urge to rest, and the raccoons were excellent storytellers.

I don't know how many days passed. I didn't care about time or days or seasons.

Every once in a while, a thought would slither into my

brain about where I was or what I was doing, but it always slithered out before I could catch it. Once it was gone, I forgot all about it until it happened again. At some point, however, I realized it was happening more frequently.

"What are you?" I asked one day as I laid on a tuft of grass, my knees bouncing against each other and my arms tucked behind my head. "Are you a garden snake? I heard they're supposed to be harmless. Are *you* harmless?"

The slithering thought didn't respond.

A beetle crawled onto my leg and begged me for a joke, so I didn't get back to the slithering thought until all my jokes were exhausted. I might have gone on forgetting about the wayward thought entirely if it hadn't slithered through my brain once more.

I found myself growing a little irritated, which was a new sensation for me. Why wouldn't the wayward thought leave me alone? Why did it want to complicate things?

"What is it you *want*, little garden snake?" I huffed, rolling onto my side so I could pluck out a few blades of grass. "Are you even supposed to be here? You're not like everyone else. You're not easy to understand, and I don't think I like you. You should leave me alone."

And so the slithering thoughts stopped for a time, and I eventually forgot all about them as I continued listening to raccoons and exchanging goofy grins with trees.

But they didn't disappear forever. They waited, patiently, until I was ready.

One day after waking from a particularly satisfying nap next to a fluffy fox, I realized that something was different. I knitted my brows together and tried to figure out what it was. The grass was still green. People still wandered around in bright clothes. A bird still hopped onto my shoulder and nuzzled me with its beak.

What could it be? Nothing's changed, even though I know something has.

I stared at my hands, studying the grooves of my skin and curvature of my nails.

I'm still me, aren't I?

I stayed that way, confused and anxious and staring at my hands, for an hour.

An hour.

Since when did I know what time was? I glanced up at the never-changing sky—and gasped! The sound was so harsh that it sent the grasshoppers into the ground and the birds skittering away to the trees.

The sun was in the west now.

It's never in the west.

My gaze, pulled down by some cosmic force I didn't understand, landed on the soft grass in front of me. There, not five feet away, stood an imposing metal door framed by nothing but sky and anxiety.

The grass shivered suddenly, and I jumped to my feet in surprise. Grass didn't move like that. The ground rumbled in response, and the sky grew dark. Delicate water droplets patted my head and tickled my ears. The wind glided across my skin, pulling the cold with it. I shivered and hugged myself.

"What is this?" I shouted to no one. "I don't understand!"

The wind turned more forceful, pushing me forward. The grass undulated back and forth, and a strange hissing noise escaped from between the blades.

Except they weren't blades of grass.

They were garden snakes.

Every single thought that had slithered into my brain

was now out in the open.

They began to move as one, wrapping around my legs and tugging me toward the daunting metal door.

"I don't want to go!" I screamed. "I'm not ready yet!"

But the winds grew fiercer, the sky hardened, and every droplet of rain stung as it slapped against my skin.

The metal door opened with a mechanical *whoosh*, and strange light poured in, obscuring my vision.

With one last collective heave, the garden snakes shoved me through the doorway.

CHAPTER TWO

SHOES DON'T TIE THEMSELVES

The other side wasn't so bad.

It took me a few minutes to get my bearings, but once I did, I felt more embarrassed than anything else.

How long did I spend in that other sphere?

I shook my head and winced. Now that I was here, it was all so obvious. I'd been cuddled and oblivious, even if the trees had smiled at me and the birds had given me hugs. It was time to move on.

Almost everyone else is already here. Am I the last to arrive?

Another cringe. I was only at the beginning, and yet I was already behind?

"Not off to a great start," I muttered.

I surveyed the sphere, absent-mindedly wiping the last of the grass blades off my legs. A beetle fell off, too, but I didn't see it.

The sky was visible, but only through large bay windows in the ceiling. The walls were white, but sometimes they changed colors when I wasn't looking. Tacky posters of kittens and videogames and inspirational quotes dotted the landscape.

I took a step forward—and nearly tripped! I glanced down. When had my shoelaces come undone?

"Hey!" a voice called in the distance. "Come over here! We're all in the queue!"

I whipped my head up, eagerly looking for the source of the voice. Blurry outlines of people stood against a wall. One was waving to me. I excitedly hurried over to join them, tripping exactly three times before I realized that shoes didn't tie themselves.

I paused in frustration and bent down to tie the laces together. When I'd finished figuring out the usefulness of bunny ears, I quickly slapped a smile on my face and looked up at the wall where the blurry outline had waved at me.

My smile slipped. They were gone. The wall was empty.

"Hey!" I yelled, sprinting toward the wall. "Where'd you all go? I'm still here!"

I reached the wall moments later, nearly slamming into it before I screeched to a halt. I thrashed my head around frantically, terrified that I'd never find them. That I'd missed my only chance.

Someone giggled in the hallway to my left.

Where did that hallway come from? Doesn't matter—I can't get left behind!

I dashed down the windowless concrete hallway, my footsteps in harmony with the sounds of laughter, ringing bells, and the shuffling of paper. But every time I thought I'd reached the blurry outlines, they disappeared right before I could join them. It didn't matter how many times I hollered at them to slow down or wait for me.

Maybe they can't hear me?

Soon the appearance of obstacles in the hallway made running difficult. Desks and chairs, books and pencils, poster board and heavy backpacks all peppered the floor.

Some were even attached to the walls, making me have to duck every so often to avoid banging my head against them. I slowed to a light jog, leaping over giant flashcards and sidestepping a dusty operating system. It wasn't long before the hallway got so crowded that I was forced to walk.

Something sharp hit me in the head, and I winced, glancing upward.

"Ow, what was that?" I muttered, gingerly rubbing the back of my head. I let out a hefty groan. The entire ceiling was covered in pencils, their pointy sides precariously jammed into the drop panels above.

"Who stores *pencils* in the *ceiling?*" I huffed as I nervously hopped out of the way of another falling pencil.

I paused, leaning against a desk overflowing with colorful page markers and plastic tabs. I rubbed my hand over my face in frustration. I was never going to catch up to them at this point. More and more junk crowded into the hallway by the minute.

"What's the point of all this?" I asked the blown-up image of a kitten trying to hang in there. I twirled around, my arms whacking against a stack of old books on one side and used juice boxes on the other. "I'm not really sure what I'm supposed to be doing. This isn't what I expected."

How did I know what to expect?

I was poised to stew indefinitely in my developing puddle of frustration, but a tantalizing *squeak* down the hallway tugged me out just in time.

"Hello?" I called. "Is anyone there?"

No one responded, of course, but I just barely glimpsed the edge of a plywood door swing open. It was slightly obscured by a set of lockers and a shiny trophy case, but I'd seen it! I hesitated for a full ten seconds before trotting toward the door. It didn't matter what was on the other side. I was getting out of this hallway.

Unfortunately, the other side of the door contained a dead-end: it was a bland room eclipsed by rows of plastic desks, the smell of pencil shavings and body odor, and small windows covered in a film of dirt and humidity. I almost didn't go in, despite my earlier convictions.

But the blurry outlines were inside the room, seated neatly behind the desks. They were talking to each other, even though I couldn't make out what they were saying. The words were muted and sounded strange.

Maybe, with time, I can learn what they are saying, learn how to talk to them.

One of the blurry shapes waved at me, and I smiled involuntarily. Before I knew it, I'd entered the room and taken a seat near the front. Another shape, taller than the rest, stood near a large, shiny board at one end of the room. The tall shape pointed toward the wall, and colors began forming in odd, wiggling patterns until the entire wall was covered with them. The tall shape moved to the next wall and pointed once more, sending colors wiggling against the blank surface. I glanced around in confusion; somehow the room had rotated to follow the tall shape, and I hadn't felt a thing.

The blurry outlines next to me *oowed* and *awed* at some of the wiggles, and a few of them even recreated the wiggles on their desks in front of them. I tried it once, pointing my finger at the surface of my own plastic desk, but nothing happened. Then I tried it twice and thrice, using a different finger and a different hand.

Nothing happened.

Meanwhile, the tall shape moved on to the next wall and the next, colors slowly spreading across the surfaces in patterns I didn't recognize.

"Excuse me?" I said quietly, raising my hand in a timid, shaky motion. The tall shape paused to stare at me. At least I think it was staring at me. I couldn't see any eyes or nose or mouth on its features. My legs bounced up and down nervously. All of the blurry outlines were looking at me now, waiting to see what I would do.

I don't like this kind of attention. I wish they'd stop.

"I-I don't understand what you're saying. Can—can you help me?"

The tall shape turned to the wall, and another spurt of colors danced across the surface in bizarre patterns. The shape gazed back at me, and I simply shook my head, feeling glum. The shape shrugged, and the other blurry outlines continued on as before. My humble efforts were not worth their consideration.

So there I sat, following wall after wall of colors wiggling against a rotating room, odd sounds hitting my ears but never venturing further into my brain, never able to make my own colors, for hours and days and years.

A sharp ring and the sound of applause tore through the room. I blinked stupidly, my brain foggy as the blurry outlines around me giggled and clapped as they formed a neat line near the door.

I cleared my throat. "Hey, where are you guys going?" I asked. My voice felt raspy from disuse.

One of the shapes waved at me, but the rest simply shrugged before resuming their garbled conversations with each other, the tittering noise jarring after staring at wiggling lights for so long.

I stood—and immediately stumbled! My legs had grown longer, and I temporarily forgot how to use them. My hands clutched the edge of my desk for support as I watched each blurry outline walk through the open door one by one.

Sweat slid down my temples as the line grew shorter and shorter.

I have to follow them! I can't get stuck here!

But my legs—my legs were sloppy mud in a storm, they were decaying pumpkins left out in the heat, bow strings someone forgot to pull taut before a concert.

"Wait!" I yelled, swinging my gaze around the room. There! The tall shape! It was still here!

"Can't you help me?" I begged it, my voice taking on

a thread of desperate pleading. "I need to follow them!"

The tall shape simply shook its head and pointed to the other side of the room toward an object I recognized. I swallowed the heavy lump in my throat.

The heavy metal door *whooshed* open, darkness blanketing the space beyond.

What happened to the light? Wasn't there light last time?

My gaze shifted to the tall shape. It was watching me, curious perhaps.

"Is this the way I have to go?" I asked softly. Part of me wanted to follow the others, even if I didn't belong with them, even if I didn't fit in wherever they were going.

The tall shape didn't say anything. It didn't even nod or shake its head. I sighed, holding back tears.

"Okay," I whispered. "I'll go."

With a grunt I shoved myself off the desk and forced my legs to wobble in the direction of the imposing metal door. Each step required far too much concentration, but eventually I made it. I paused at the door's entrance, but I didn't look back, even though I'd miss the wiggling colors and the one blurry outline that'd waved at me.

Chapter Three

Forks

I found myself in a circular chamber of sorts. As soon as the door behind me *whooshed* close, I shut my eyes and sucked in a large breath.

"Wow," I breathed loudly. "*That* sphere was a doozy." My eyes popped open as I surveyed the chamber around me. "I think I'll pick something easier this time."

A huge window stretched vertically around the diameter of the sphere, separating two different sets of large metal doors. The whole sphere was composed of white, gray, and black metal, with a touch of reinforced glass here and there. Nothing but inky black space was visible beyond the sphere's windows.

"I must be on one of the peripheral spheres." I sighed. "Too bad I can't see the rest of the station. Then I could at least get an idea of where *these* doors lead."

The four doors glistened in the sphere's artificial light. Nothing distinguished them from each other. I couldn't even tell if there was another pathway back to this crossroad. Did I have to choose a door at random? What if I never got back? Would I ever know what was behind those other doors?

I shifted my weight. "It'd be nice if they put a bench or something in here. I don't know how long it'll take me to make up my mind."

But I knew they would never put a bench in here. They didn't want people lingering or dawdling.

I scuffed my boot against the metal flooring, the small sound echoing around the empty chamber.

"Okay! Okay. I'll just pick one, right? It's better if I don't know. Hmm—let's see. How about . . . that one!" I stomped confidently toward the center right door. "Yes, this is the one! I can feel it!"

The metal door *whooshed* open at my approach, blinding white light engulfing me. I winced, shielding my eyes with my hands. I stumbled over the entrance, but the light graciously disappeared as soon as I was through.

Chapter Four

Singing Fish

Infinite darkness. A black metal floor. No breeze.

Slowly, distant sights and sounds filtered into my awareness. There, just in front of me, I could hear familiar voices talking to each other. Catchy music floated around the voices, their words somehow meshing with the tune perfectly, like it was all planned.

After a few minutes, the voices morphed into shapes, but they were distorted. I tilted my head, frowning.

"Oh!" I finally said. I walked forward and pivoted. "There we go! I wasn't looking at it right."

Sure enough, now that I was facing the moving image directly, I had no trouble seeing or hearing it. People moved around a living room, talking about their work and love interests and conspiring to do something crazy yet oddly endearing.

A hidden audience laughed at their jokes. I laughed, too.

I stood there, watching the other people as they accomplished things and failed, as they connected and fought, as they went through life but always ended up back at square one.

My chest clenched uncomfortably. I backed away from the people. They were sitting on their couch, chatting as usual, and they didn't say goodbye when I left.

What am I supposed to do now?

I felt drained, but hungry for more. What else was there? I glanced around the room.

"Oh!" I said, startled. Behind me was another group of people, but these people were fighting with rays of light and leaping over rivers and plunging into canyons. "This looks exciting. I'll stay here for a bit."

And so I did. I stayed there, watching the new group of people move in unrealistic ways and use laws of physics that surely couldn't exist. I stayed until my eyes began drifting to the edges of their existence, until I no longer cared about every word they said, until the catchy music became more annoying than fun.

A headache was forming between my temples, stretching out across every rivulet of gray and white matter between them. My eyes watered, and I yawned, backing away from the people as they dashed across rooftops.

Another swirl of voices and colors caught my gaze, but I shook my head. "Not again. Not right now."

However, a few steps later, I found myself watching cute dogs looking abashed while their owners chuckled from beside me. I chucked, too.

And then there were cats falling off surfaces and licking ice cream and hissing in the most adorable way.

And then came the people singing acapella to my favorite song. And my other favorite song. And my *other* favorite song.

I gasped at the monsoon waters rushing down a boulevard crowded with cars, I scoffed at the ridiculous argument people were having, I laughed at the minimalist drawing of someone unsuccessfully trying to get out of bed.

Every time I pulled away, I found another reason to get back in.

They were everywhere, behind me, beside me, no matter which direction I walked.

Days—maybe weeks?—passed before I even realized what I was doing.

I was so tired.

And sad.

I was surrounded by people and things and places, yet I'd never felt more consciously aware of my own intense loneliness. I'd been pumped full of thoughts, feelings, ideas, and possibilities—and then promptly drained of everything. Again and again.

Where am I in all of this?

I saw and experienced everything but myself. There was no time for that, no emotional or mental room for the one *self* that I had.

My shoulder slumped against a cold, metal corner, and I finally managed to close my eyes. Words and music drifted in from a group of anthropomorphized fish in front of me. The fish were singing and going to school.

I'd learned by now that every direction held something new, and no direction held nothing.

It would be so easy to stay here forever.

But I would never be happy again if I did.

Something sparked inside me, a little whisp of a pungent feeling, and an inkling of resolve edged its way from my heart to my brain, my spine, my toes. With a herculean effort my eyes flitted open, and with another herculean effort I kept my eyes from latching onto the singing fish and getting pulled into their world.

For the first time, I could *see* where I was. The floor, the ceiling, and every wall were all made of a heartless black metal, each panel chilly and indifferent. The only light came from the many worlds that begged for my attention. These worlds were supported, or perhaps embedded, in the walls, each one separated by only a few centimeters. I'd listened to so many of them. There should have been a cacophony of noise, but the discord would have been too strong to pull anyone in. No, it was designed so that the viewer could only hear the world in front of them.

Clever. Purposeful.

Sadistic.

I blinked every few seconds, urging my brain to remain steadfast. If I Lost myself again . . .

"No," I rasped.

My throat was dry, my tongue swollen.

"No," I said again.

I'd wanted to make sure I'd really said it the first time.

"No."

Firmer than before.

"No!"

Resolution.

My hand shoved my arm away from the wall, bringing life into the rest of my corpse. My joints ached, my stomach curved inward, and I couldn't remember which world I'd left my muscles in.

I wanted to leave. Now, all I had to do was figure out how.

The wall in front of me curved to the left. I followed it, eyes cast either downward or upward to avoid the worlds that beckoned me with open arms. My moral tenacity was, therefore, the cause of my smashing my skull into a rather stiff wall.

I sucked in a pained breath as an awkward *clang* mingled with the tears of a young girl. I made the mistake of glancing at the girl, her brown pigtails wobbling against her shaking shoulders. Her mother was in a coma. Her father had been murdered. Now it was up to two at-odds detectives to bring justice to the situation. It was touch and go for them. They always seemed to be one step behind the mastermind, and, of course, it was about more than just a single murder. Right when it seemed most hopeless, the detectives pulled through, shrewd as they were, and everyone was safe. I sighed in relief, happy for them and proud that evil hadn't triumphed.

My eye twitched.

Catchy, purposeful music pinged my ears. The detectives were back. Something else was wrong, and only they could help.

My teeth gnawed at the inside of my cheek.

Oh no! It was another secret conspiracy against the helpless! How were the detectives going to get out of this mess?

My knees buckled, and my whole body went limp. An elbow banged against the floor. My nose whacked into my knees. I lay there, hating how my body smarted, but welcoming the sensations that were my own.

It happened again. I was Lost.

Despair threatened to melt my limbs into the floor

panels, but a single realization staved it off.

Somehow, I'd know what was happening that time, and I'd pulled myself out of it.

I *did that. And* I *could do it again.*

Slowly, grudgingly, my limbs propped themselves up, my vertebrae got back in line, and my nose stopped complaining about its new crimson curtain.

My eyes followed the outline of the floor until it met the curvature of the wall I'd run into.

"What?" I said, startled, mouth falling open. "It's a dead end?"

I spun in a circle, careful not to focus on any world for too long. My lips pursed.

"It's a dead end. *Why?* There's nothing down here, except for more worlds."

I walked back the way I'd come, my footsteps tapping against the black metal floor. I reached the corner with the singing fish, but there was no other passageway, just the same hallway further back the way I'd come. Frowning, I continued backward until the hallway opened into a room with two other hallways. I didn't remember seeing the other hallways before, but sure enough there was the hissing cat and the abashed dog. I accidentally watched the cat for a while before the feeling of my fingers tugging on my earlobe brought me back to the present.

I blinked rapidly and focused on the uninspiring metal panel above me.

"At least it was quicker this time. *And* less painful."

I wiped some of the dried blood off my nose.

My legs took me to one of the other hallways at random, and I followed the unrelenting tunnel until it, too, apexed in a dead end. I was pleased that I'd only gotten Lost three times on the whole journey there and back, albeit one of those lasted much longer than I was proud of.

Part of me wanted to go back that way, to take my time and enjoy all the worlds I was missing.

Instead, my legs took me down a different hallway.

This path was just as crowded as the others, family holidays and drama spilling over into gazelles in the safari before making waves with surfer kids and time machines. I got Lost on a journey to the center of a planet, but I made it back before the dinosaurs could eat me.

After wading through a marsh during the civil

war—the civil war between robots and humans, that is—I finally turned a bend to discover a split in the hallway.

"Which way should I go?" I asked a talking parrot as he coasted through a forest of lush trees. "Left or right?"

"Right!" The parrot squawked loudly.

I eyed the parrot shrewdly, wondering if this was some sort of trick. "Right, you say?"

"Right, you say!" confirmed the parrot before he dipped into the trees and out of my line of sight.

"Hmm. Do I trust the parrot?"

I stared at the trees. I stared at the diverging hallways.

Finally, I sighed. "Right it is, then."

And Right I went. I followed Right until Right led me to another Left and another Right.

Unfortunately, there was no talking parrot at this intersection.

My foot tapped impatiently on the metal floor. *Tap. Tap. Tap.*

"Right?" I asked myself, testing the waters. "No. Yes? Yes, I think Right still feels right."

It wasn't.

I reached the end of the corridor, fought off a bridezilla

and her entourage, and sprinted all the way back to the intersection, turning down the other pathway without any hesitation.

"So, it's not always Right, is it?" I muttered to myself.

How will I ever figure out all these rules? There're too many, and they don't make any sense.

I followed Left until it dumped me out into a network of *three* other hallways. Three!

I spent the next week figuring out that neither Left nor Right could help me. Only the center corridor led somewhere that, in turn, led somewhere else.

This was all I did, all I *could* do. Stumble and try. Fail and try again.

Sometimes, I barely kept myself from getting Lost as I wandered through the maze of endless hallways, and every time I got stuck, pillars of shame smashed into my diaphragm.

However . . . I wasn't completely Lost. And each time I felt like I was a little more in control.

Except I wasn't.

This maze was tailored for me, and the further into the maze I went, the more relatable every world became.

It could all be mine. It *was* all mine.

Except it wasn't.

These weren't *my* experiences. These weren't my friends, my pets, my family. I didn't live in that house or apartment. I had no special powers or apex skills. A robot didn't raise me. I wasn't invincible. I didn't own that wardrobe or drive that car.

These worlds weren't mine, despite how much they felt like they were.

And so, each time I got Lost, I found a way out, my tiny spark of resolve molding and growing into something new. Every diverging hallway, every dead end, every corridor carried me further out of the maze. I could have turned around, gone out the way I'd come in, but then I wouldn't have made any progress. I'd still be *that* me, not *this* me.

Step after step. Deciding and following and backtracking and deciding again.

Until one day, when I made my final turn. There, the hallway suddenly ended, and all that was left was infinite darkness and a black metal floor. A breeze blew lightly across my face, and I sighed in contentment, my eyes drifting shut.

The *whoosh* of the door opening blended with the cool breeze. My eyes opened slowly, taking in the darkness beyond the door.

I walked through without another thought.

Chapter Five

Forks and Spoons

The door led me back to the large open chamber with four other metal doors, as I'd known it would as soon as I'd seen the darkness on the other side. Of course, I would have gone through the door even if I hadn't known where it led. Anything to leave *that* sphere behind. I shuddered as recent memories unwillingly floated through my brain.

"That sphere *was* easier, in some ways," I said to the open, empty room. "But not in the way I wanted. I . . . I don't ever want to go through something like that again."

I walked to the center of the sphere, eyes wandering to the inky black space visible just beyond the long, vertical windows.

I still want to see the rest of the station, but I also

wouldn't mind a view of a moon or planet. I'd even take a glimpse of a blurry, nearly-dispersed nebula.

The sound of a throat clearing startled me, and I spun around the room looking for the source.

The room was empty.

I realized, with a start, that *I'd* been the one to clear my throat.

"Now that's an uncomfortable sensation," I said. My voice laughed with fake emotion, the kind someone used when they were trying to lighten a tense or unnerving situation.

"I *am* unnerved," I muttered to myself. "How dissociated from myself did I become in that sphere?" My heart rate sped up, and I began pacing around the sphere. "I don't even know how long I was in there, but it wasn't like the other spheres. This wasn't pleasant. I-I need a break, I think. Somewhere relaxing, where I can gather myself together again."

I peered at the three unknown doors. Did any of them lead to such a place? Or would I end up in some tormented realm, Lost again?

"I suppose I could stay here for a while." I glanced

around the sphere and sighed. "If only there was a bench or something . . ."

The metal floor looked cold and uninviting, and the walls of the sphere curved in such a way that I'd be hunched over if I tried to lean against them. I sighed and laid down on the floor, right in the middle of the sphere.

Nothing moved beyond the windows. Nobody entered or exited through the doors. The only sounds were my ragged breathing and the occasional rustle of my pant leg against the cool floor.

Minutes passed, but I didn't feel any better.

"Nope, I don't think this is doing it," I said, sitting up. I studied the three remaining unknown doors, wondering what kinds of experiences they led to.

"It's such a risk, to just pick one at random. Look at what happened last time," I reasoned to myself. "However," I countered, not one to be deterred forever, "I *do* have to pick something. Or go back. These are my options right now." Another sigh. "I just wish I had a bit of insight. Anything to point me in the right direction."

I waited, glancing around the sphere for a hint or clue to suddenly emerge. My leg fell asleep, but that was the only thing that happened. I stood, stamping out the pins and needles.

"I suppose that's my sign," I muttered. "Can't hover in indecision forever. Fine! I'll go random again."

And so I lumbered over to the door on the far left, shielded my eyes from the blinding white light as it *whooshed* open, and walked through.

CHAPTER SIX

TALKING WRENS

C rickets chirped as pockets of air twirled gently between deciduous leaves. Dew fragranced the soil, and eudicot flowers scented the dancing air. Easy daffodil sunlight tickled my face as monarchs and blue morphos glided over a field of verdant bluegrass spotted with vibrant birches, beeches, oaks, dogwoods, and maples.

"Wow," I breathed. "What is this place?"

Wrens, thrushes, and warblers answered me lazily as they chitchatted in the tree branches.

I padded through the lush field, admiring the spurts of coneflowers, columbines, and milkweeds nestled next to sturdy trunks. The dogwoods were blooming, the tender breeze scattering their delicate pink petals across the landscape.

It would be so easy to stay here forever.

And I might be happy again if I did.

I sat down next to an oak, leaning into its stalwart bark. The soft grass welcomed me with a plush embrace. The conscientious breeze sent blushing petals and evaporated oils in my direction, bestowing a sweet aroma that eased the tension from my muscles. The sun never wavered, its warmth perfectly calculated to neither overchill nor overheat.

I don't know how long I stayed there, admiring and observing the calm landscape. Birds flitted about, their poignant songs trailing after them. Bees sampled each flower, the timid wind only strong enough to make the leaves sing and the blades of grass sway in a hypnotic rhythm.

At some point I shifted, laying down in the soft grass. Now the oak's canopy was visible in a whole new way, with streaks of blue sky and cumulus clouds weaving around the jubilant leaves and meandering branches. The squirrels and the warblers held a casual conclave while ants marched and grasshopper nymphs munched on plump foliage. I didn't speak for hours, simply wanting to exist as just another piece of the serene landscape.

My mind was clearer than it had ever been before, and I finally understood what peace truly was.

A wren landed on my leg some hours later, cocking its drab brown head toward me. A dowdy white stripe extended over its eyes to the front of its head, and its belly was, at best, a dull yellow. The wren, perhaps to spite its unspectacular appearance, opened its beak and began to chirp and whistle in strong and fluid tones, each note a lively call that transformed its brown into rich soil, its white into cirrus wisps, and its yellow into dew-sprinkled lemons. I could only stare, transfixed, as it shared its stories with me.

When the tiny wren finally paused for breath, I jumped at my chance to return the favor, to share some of myself with it.

"Hello," I began excitedly. "Do you want to know my name? Where I come from? Who my family and friends are?"

The wren tilted its head the other way but remained silent.

My wide smile drooped slightly. "How about why I'm

here? What I do?"

The little wren hopped up my leg and perched on my knee, but it still didn't say anything.

"I'll take that as a yes?" I asked, my voice painfully hopeful. "I'm a traveler, of sorts. And I'm here on this space station to—"

The wren suddenly flapped its short wings and volleyed upward through the air. It joined a group of other wrens on the oak's largest branch, and the chime immediately exchanged chirps and *tuks* and a few *jimmy jimmy's*.

A fragment of my peace flew away with the taciturn wren. My mouth hung open, and a tear threatened to punch its way out of my left duct.

It didn't care. Not at all. I listened, and I loved it, and it didn't even care.

The wrens continued to gossip, and I forced myself to look away. I focused on the soft grass, on the worms that wiggled in the soil and the snails that clung to the wobbling blades. I breathed in the sweet air around the wildflowers and dogwood petals, and I watched the condensed water vapor coalesce in the sky.

After a few minutes, the wren's rejection no longer stung. "Now I can get back to relaxing and enjoying myself," I said confidently. I leaned back against the oak, but the bark wasn't as welcoming as I remembered. The trunk was just a sturdy and stalwart as before—that hadn't changed—but . . . perhaps my view of the tree had shifted. I stood, suddenly uncomfortable with these feelings.

I surveyed the swaying field and the fresh trees around me. "A walk would be nice," I decided. My legs carried me to every tree, around every flower, and by every singing bird. Each step imbued a sliver of peace back into the empty cavern behind my sternum.

More time passed as I allowed the landscape to smooth out my sharp edges and fill the pockets of vacuum in my psyche. I tried talking to the warblers and thrushes, but they were just as disinterested as the wren had been. The crickets and grasshoppers felt the same way, as did the worms and the bees. The trees were always available, but they lacked the warmth I craved.

One day, after spending the morning watching the sunlight scatter across the atmosphere, I realized—with both relief and heartbreak—that I had to keep moving.

This wonderful place had restored me, but I couldn't stay here forever. I was comfortable, but there was more to life than being comfortable. I was lonely, despite being surrounded by life. There was life but no love.

I walked through the field, gingerly stepping around the coneflowers and milkweeds. I glanced back at the landscape, inhaling the delicate sweet scents, and waved goodbye to the trees and grass and birds. A door *whooshed* open behind me, but I didn't turn around just yet. The breeze picked up speed, sending the leaves into a mad chorus. Then the warblers and thrushes and even the wrens joined in, harmonizing with the dancing leaves and the swaying blades of gentle grass. The sunlight dripped through the sky, reverberating around the swooping clouds, decorating each chloroplast in the field with beads of gold.

I smiled as the single tear finally leaked out. Only then did I turn and step through the metal door.

CHAPTER SEVEN

FORKS AND SPOONS AND KNIVES

The empty metal sphere felt bleak after the lively landscape. My heart threatened to sink, but I yanked it up, determined to keep going, to keep experiencing.

That's the point of the space station, after all.

... Isn't it?

I lifted my head, expecting to see the same set of four doors in front of me. My eyes widened. Instead of four large metal doors, there were just two, and each was framed by wide vertical windows that showcased an exploded nebula.

Fractals of cosmic dust swirled outward from the

neutron core of the once-dazzling star. Teals and maroons and deep greens that slipped into yellow skirted across the black expanse, luminous tendrils reaching inward and outward, glorious webs and globules combining with infinite precision.

The supernova death spread out far beyond the windows' capacity. I pushed myself up against the thick glass, desperate to see more, but even plastered against the icy window I couldn't see the edges of the nebula.

"How could something like this—something so big, so wonderful—exist?" I said, my warm breath fogging the glass.

I admired the nebula for a while, trying to soak in its stellar details—every curl of its cosmic swirls, every burst of color from the dissipating clouds of hydrogen, helium, carbon, nitrogen, and oxygen. I knew I'd never see something quite like it again.

An annoying *beep beep beep* sounded through the sphere, and I jumped back from the window in surprise. The noise persisted, and I swiveled my head around the room, looking for an explanation. There were no visible speakers, and no red "danger" lights spun around the room.

That's good, at least. But what's going on?

"Hello?" I called, raising my voice to be heard above the *beep beep Beep*. "Is there something wrong with the station?"

I couldn't imagine that anything short of twin black holes would affect the space station, but even then they'd likely find a way out of the catastrophic mess.

The *Beep Beep Beep* blasted against my skull.

Is it getting louder?

"Hey!" I shouted, spinning around the room. "Can someone shut this off and explain to me what's going on?"

I sprinted over to the door I'd just walked through. It didn't *whoosh* open at my approach. I tucked that uncomfortable thought away for later and banged my fist against the door, calling out again to the unresponsive station moderators.

Nervous tension built in my stomach, and I backed away from the door, eyeing the two unknown doors. Would they open if I approached? Or would they remain tightly shut, the whole space station in lockdown?

I gulped, sorely hoping there wasn't anything wrong

with the station. I didn't think I'd get out in time if there was.

The alarm was definitely getting louder, doing wonders to my blood pressure. I ran over to the two metal doors, stopping in front of the one on the right.

It *whooshed* open as I neared it, sending streaks of white light into the sphere. I sighed loudly, relief helping to temper my surging blood pressure.

At least I'm not stuck in here.

I almost walked through the gapping door, but I hesitated. I stepped over to the other door, and it too *whooshed* open.

"They both work," I mused, but I could hardly hear myself over the escalating *BEEP BEEP BEEP*.

Left or Right?

The parrot had said Right, but Right wasn't always right. Neither was Left. But Right had worked before when I'd had to make a choice. Swallowing my unease, I dashed toward the Right door and into the white light.

CHAPTER EIGHT

MIRRORS

The alarm's incessant tone had not followed me, thankfully. That was the good news. I had planned to blindly run through this next sphere, hoping to get to another crossroads sphere where someone on the station could make sure everything was fine.

I should have known better.

There was no running through the spheres. No shortcuts. Even now, thoughts of the alarm were already dissipating from my conscious self.

And then they were gone.

As my foot crossed the barrier, I immediately and overwhelming knew one thing: Everyone in here was better than me.

Gold and silver tinkled together, bright jewels glinted off every polished surface, and so much confidence, elegance, charisma, experience, and knowledge were stuffed into the air that I found it mildly difficult to breathe. My chest heaved, my lungs trying to filter out everything I couldn't handle, everything that was above my capability.

A women laughed behind me; the decibels, length, and intonation were all chosen with excruciating perfection.

A man walked by, and I couldn't help but stare. His gate was flawless. I didn't know someone could *walk* flawlessly. It shouldn't matter. It was just a walk.

Why should it matter how someone walks?

But then I took another step forward. It was only one step, and yet I was hit with the weight of just how *imperfect* my step was. It shouldn't matter. It was just a step.

So I stood where I was, rooted in place by my fear of imperfection. No, not a fear of imperfection. Rather, a fear of everyone here seeing the total extent of my flaws, flaws in a place where no flaws lived. I wasn't simply another quirk amongst a sea of quirks. I was the cracked keystone decorating the floor between pillars of a colosseum, long fallen and deemed obsolete. Inadequate.

Another woman walked by. Her hair was both shiny and full, not a split end in sight. Its shades and hues were an intoxicating blend of uniqueness and docility. Her makeup, clothes, jewelry—everything was complimentary, a complete outfit expertly arranged and worn with a level of proficiency I had never before witnessed.

I don't know how long I stood there, frozen, my senses bombarded by perfection made incarnate. People continued to walk by, and I continued to stare, unable to stop myself. Awareness slowly drizzled through my scalp and into my gray matter, and I finally made myself turn around.

The door was gone. I'd expected as much, though. It seemed I no longer had the option to go back.

What if I'd never had that option to begin with?

My stomach rolled, and my breath hitched.

Would the station moderators lie to me like that? I thought—

A delicate waterfall descended from the ceiling,

cascading in gentle waves down the wall in front of me. An elaborate koi pond with rough-strewn stone formed just beyond my feet, and all thoughts of the station sunk beneath the glittering scales of pearl and agate.

The Perfects were soon drawn to the pond and its inhabitants of good fortune. Men and women—if they were even still human—sat and stood in selective poses around the carp home. I adverted my eyes before the scene wrecked my brain from sensory overload. The concentration of Perfects was too saturated, the colors too vibrant, the sweets scents of jasmine and the musky urban cologne too cloying.

I kept my head down and walked further into the room. I needed to move away, even if I didn't know where I was going. After several minutes of lumbering and ungainly steps on my part, a black marble bench poised against a carnelian and sapphire column caught my eye, and I instantly threw myself on top, grateful to have a place to sit and orient myself.

The marble was deliciously cool, and I allowed the briskness to clear away the effervescent shine of the Perfects from my senses. I concentrated on the room itself, forcing my brain to focus on something besides the Perfects. My eyes found the floor first, settling on the feature that required the least resistance to gravity.

The expansive floor was smooth and reflective, like polished concrete or ancient stone, with dark clouds obscuring treasure troves of jewels and rivers of otherworldly light. Columns grew out of the floor like water flowing upward, their surfaces utterly flawless, and they continued up and up into black and gold vapors that stagnantly occupied the heavens. Between the columns were strange geometric shapes in pastel colors, at odds with the dark Grecian glory of the room. The shapes would shift when I wasn't watching, morphing from an icosahedron into a pentagonal prism in the span of a blink. Some of the Perfects observed the shapes with awe; others lounged against them like they were Egyptian chaises.

Hours passed before my mind adapted to the crushing, near-alien perfection around me. I could finally observe the Perfects without instant oblivion, without instant disgust at my own existence.

No, that's still there. You're just pretending it's not.

I began to notice the same Perfects walking around

or reclining on the strange pastel shapes, but they would be wearing different clothes, or have a new hair style. Not a minute later, the same Perfects would stroll by, a completely new look attached to their corporeal flawlessness.

Finally, identical Perfects crossed paths—one wearing a daisy button-down and sun-kissed hair, and the other midnight locks pinned back over a sleeveless linen tank—and I gasped, the realization sinking in.

There wasn't just one of each Perfect, there were *dozens!* Each with the same face but scattered throughout the room like mirror images, giving the illusion that each was exclusive and distinct.

These people— *Were they clones? Phantoms?*—dotted the landscape of the radiant columns and spectral floor, spread out like wildflowers in a field but with diamonds and rubies instead of petals and stamens. Some of these Mirrors sported different clothes, donned different jewelry, clutched different bags. Some Mirrors stood shoulder to shoulder with others, almost touching. Others stood far away. Some laughed, some argued, some cried.

Yet whatever they did, they did it perfectly.

The Mirrors were Perfects, and it was impossible to tell who was the real one, if they were all real, or if any of them were real to begin with.

As I remained resolutely fixed to the cool marble bench, studying the Perfects, an odd pattern began to form out of the corner of my eye, something that tugged at my vision when I glanced this way or that. After a few tries, I finally realized what was so unnerving.

Some Mirrors stopped doing anything at all unless I was looking at them. They stood stonelike, paused in whatever action they'd been doing. What they did held no meaning unless I was watching them.

Why? I'm imperfect. Why do they need someone like me to see them?

I had no answers. The Perfects might know, though. Fear raced through me at the thought of speaking to one of them, but I didn't know what else to do in this place. I could only watch for so long without engaging.

My nerve evaporated as a lithe and willowy woman danced around a column, but it reformed again in time to ask the next Perfect that strode by. His hair was a deep brown and spiked on one side in an artful manner, and his toned body was barely hidden beneath some kind of sleeveless, gold-trimmed mediation robe that fell to his feet yet hugged his every curve.

I opened my mouth, but the words ran into each other in the back of my throat. "I–c–could–you–were–why?" I rasped unintelligibly. The Perfect glanced at me. He smiled but raised an eyebrow, confusion glimmering behind his vibrant eyes.

My tongue was dry, and the words seemed to stick and break when they crossed over the rough surface. "I–I, well you—that is, um." I closed my eyes and took a deep breath. "Why—why do you need—" I waved my hand around the room "—this? And—" I pointed to myself "—and me?"

The Perfect stopped, his attention fully on me. Faint crinkles of confusions lined his forehead as he peered around the room. "This? And you?" he finally said, mimicking my hand waving, albeit in more elegant motions that I was capable of.

I nodded, not trusting my vocal cords.

The Perfect tilted his head, and several brown locks tumbled to the side. "This? And you?" he repeated. "That's all there is."

Now it was my turn to frown. "N-no," I said, proud of my minimal stuttering. "There's e-everything else, too. Not just *This*."

He smiled, and I choked on the radiance of the simple action.

"*This* is all that matters. So *This* is all there is," he stated, his tone somehow playful and serious at the same time.

The Perfect's Mirror strode in front of him, but he didn't acknowledge the other him in any way.

Do they know there are Mirrors of themselves?

My frown deepened. "Did—did you see him?" I pointed to the Mirror. "It's you!"

The Perfect followed my outstretched hand, his smile never slipping.

"I see nothing," he chimed, his voice more melodic than before.

My lips parted. "W-what? But—but it's you!" I glanced back at the Mirror. He looked stunning in a black-tie suit, his curly hair slicked back, with a single black rose in his hand. His hips were swaying to a tango only he could hear.

"Look!" I shouted at the Perfect in front of me. "You're dancing! In a suit!"

The Perfect's eyes shone in recognition. "Ah! You've seen me dance! How wonderful." The Perfect turned and started walking away.

"Wait!" I shouted, frustration mixing with my muddled thoughts.

The Perfect briefly glanced over his shoulder, winked, and said, "I hope you'll see my other dances." Then he continued walking away, and I knew it was pointless to run after him demanding more answers.

The Perfect's inability to see his Mirror niggled at me. How was that possible? Were they all the same, or were they connected by a hive mind of sorts?

Do I have any Mirrors?

It was a brief thought. A quick glance around the room revealed that I was the only *me* here.

How can I get a Mirror? Do I want a Mirror?

Perhaps if I had a Mirror, I would be a little more perfect, like everyone else in here.

Should I want that? To be like them?

I had no clue. Yet the fact that I didn't understand who

these Mirrors were and where they came from proved to me that I had no business with them. I would leave the Mirrors to the Perfects, where they belonged.

I slumped against the cool marble bench, perplexed, and decided to pass the time by simply watching the Perfects and their Mirrors. I stayed that way until my neck stiffened. I shifted and drooped into a different position, laying there until my back spasmed. I repeated this ritual three more times until nearly every part of my body ached in some form or fashion. My eyes were bloodshot and dry, and a trembling headache throbbed beneath my temples. My body threatened sleep but never carried through. Fatigue overwhelmed me, yet my muscles protested loudly from disuse. My consciousness floated in limbo, and I feared I would never be free of this tormented state. The Perfects kept walking by, none-the-wiser to my disintegrating shell.

A timid memory tickled my cerebellum. My legs twitched in response.

I've been Lost before. Lost and unable to stop being Lost.

Despair bloomed in my rib cage, but something delicate yet strong pushed it back.

I've been Lost . . . but I found a way out. There is always a way out.

Before I knew what I was doing, my body sprang up, sending blood rushing to forgotten corners and leaving my head swimming in opaque vision. I braced a hand against the column, breathing hard until the stars and fog disappeared.

A few Perfects glanced at my sudden movement, but they quickly forgot about me. The others didn't even notice my strange behavior.

"Hey!" I yelled, suddenly angry.

Not one Perfect looked at me.

"Hey! Look at me!" I shouted, clenching my hands. A few Perfects altered their paths to avoid me, but otherwise none of them acknowledged me.

"I know you can hear me! I talked to one of you!"

Silence.

I jogged around the room, avoiding columns and pastel geometry, as I shoved myself in front of one Perfect after another, forcing them to see me. Each one tilted their head or looked over their shoulder—anything to avoid my gaze.

"You can't ignore me forever!" I said, my voice screeching.

Desperate, I reached for a Perfect's arm, hoping the sudden touch would jostle her into acknowledging me. Just before my fingers gripped her smooth skin, the Perfect shimmered and suddenly disappeared. My mouth flopped open.

"How did you do that?" I whispered, whirling around. "Where did you go?"

I ran over to another Perfect. "Did you see that? She disappeared!"

The Perfect smiled at me, her almond eyes glinting in sympathy. "It's just an effect. You know that."

I shook my head vigorously. "No, I don't! Why are you all ignoring me?"

The Perfect smoothed out her flowing satin dress. "Your ruckus act makes us uneasy. Have you tried anything else?"

"My what?" I pulled at my hair, feeling unhinged.

The Perfect frowned, her small nose scrunching slightly. "No, no I don't think this will do either." She shrugged and walked away. "Oh well, you'll figure something out."

"Where are you going?" I shouted at her squared shoulders. She glanced back, tossing her lush hair behind her and sending faint whisps of spring cherries in my direction. Her scrutinizing eyes appraised me, and I could feel her scanning me cell by cell, thread by thread.

Finally, she shrugged again. "Maybe we can collaborate in the future. I'm all full with other projects right now, I'm afraid." She smiled, the brilliance of it halting my incessant questions. "Best of luck, of course."

I stared after her until she faded into the sea of Perfects.

Why don't I know what she's talking about?

I heard the words the Perfects spoke, but they held no meaning for me. They were as alien as the Perfects and their Mirrors. I could stay and try to understand them, and I felt that, with time, I would.

Another memory niggled at me of a place with swirling voices and wiggling colors and of not belonging. The difference was that I *could* belong here, with enough time and practice. I could mold myself into the right shapes or learn to mimic the empyrean floor or the sinuous columns. Maybe one day, I'd even have Mirrors of my own. I could *make* this place mine.

But I'd have to give up something along the way.

Would it be growth or rot? There was no way to tell.

But I'd lose something, something I wasn't sure I wanted to part with.

And I'd only be doing it to fit in; I didn't know if This was what I wanted.

A distant warbling song echoed off the columns, and my breath hitched in my throat. A warm breeze tickled my skin, and earthen scents of fresh soil and aged bark embraced me for a single second.

Then they were gone.

And suddenly I remembered that there was more than This.

I turned on my heel, striding toward the back of the room and far, far away from the sprinkling waterfall and the glittering scales of luck. The Perfects watched me go, their smiles flawless. I knew they didn't care one way or the other if I stayed or went, but still they watched.

My tread soon broke into a jog then a sprint as I dashed for the end. I wasn't escaping; I was *striving*. Each unwieldy step pounded in harsh slaps against the floor, perfect replicas swimming up to meet my feet in the floor's reflection. Onward and onward I ran, beads of sweat forming on my hairline. Columns curved out of my way, and pastel shapes rolled away from my flopping legs.

At last, the dark clouds above shimmered with more gold than ink, and no columns or prisms ventured this far. I slowed to a walk, panting as I glanced behind me. Like an alpine tree line, the Perfects and their Mirrors didn't venture beyond the last chartreuse and emerald column or the last chalk-blue cube.

They were all watching, eyes glued to me like soulless robots.

Then, as one, they turned and marched back into the depths of their ethereal world.

A mechanical *whoosh* sent a fresh breeze across my skin. It was sterile and devoid of earth, but I was perfectly fine with that.

The sound of glass rubbing on glass clattered behind me, and I looked back toward the open door and the white light streaming through. Between me and the door lay a bed of glittering gems, the light from the door magnifying their colors tenfold.

Spontaneously, I reached down and plucked an oversized emerald and ruby from the jeweled rug, pocketing them for later.

"Might as well get something for my efforts," I muttered.

I smoothed out my hair and wiped invisible grime from my sleaves. The closer I got to the door, the more I felt like I was waking up from a hazy dream. There were so many colors in the dream, but the logic didn't always make sense, and, in the end, it would be better to be out of it where I could think more clearly and exist more clearly.

I stepped through the door.

CHAPTER NINE

PAPER TAPESTRIES: PART ONE

My next step found only air, and my body tumbled forward before I could stop myself. My eyes closed of their own accord as I fell, waiting for the impact to come. When several seconds passed with only air tugging at my hair and clothes, my eyes shot open in surprise.

I was floating through a baby blue sky like a feather with low air resistance. Picturesque clouds, fluffier than cotton balls, drifted by. I dared to look down—and then wished I hadn't! I screamed on instinct as a never-ending landscape of rolling green hills undulated beneath me, the hills getting closer and closer by the second. I was skydiving with no gravity cuffs or parachute.

It didn't matter that my body had suddenly adopted the mass and surface area of a feather. I was still falling too fast.

Five hundred feet.

Something large wiggled uncomfortably in my pocket.

Four hundred feet.

I screamed again, for lack of anything else to do.

Two hundred feet.

I gasped as something sharp poked my thigh. I reached in my pocket, pulling out the hefty emerald and ruby. They gleamed tauntingly at me.

One hundred feet.

I was going to die, and palm-sized gems couldn't save me.

Fifty feet.

Desperate, and as a last Hail Mary from my stupidity, I chucked the emerald and ruby at the ground beneath me.

Ten feet.

Fueled by my extra thrust, the gems thudded against the ground before I did. They hit the short grass and rolled away.

Nothing happened.

I shoved my arms over my eyes, knowing it wouldn't help me.

Then I hit the ground.

A thunderous *SSHHHKK* and *RRRIIPP* echoed through my bones, and suddenly I was falling again. I glanced up in confusion, just in time to see the ground above me ripped apart like a massive paper tapestry where I had fallen through. The baby blue sky and cotton ball clouds surrounded me once more, and another set of undulating hills swam hundreds of feet below my plummeting body.

"Not again!" I yelled. My adrenaline spiked once more, but a tiny part of me inexplicably relaxed. If I hadn't died the last time, then perhaps I wouldn't die this time either.

But will I be stuck in a never-ending loop of falling? How am I supposed to get out of here?

Glittering specks of green then red fell through the rip in the ground above. The green speck dove past me, but the red one smacked me in the head before bouncing off and chasing after its nicer partner.

"Ow!" I winced, rubbing my head as I sliced through

the air.

The emerald and ruby spun around each other like exotic dancers, gaining speed with every yard they fell. They shot through the air with such force that they surely must have pushed beyond their maximum velocities, despite the impossibility of such a feat.

While I was still five hundred feet—give or take—above the rolling hills, the gems struck the ground like meteors, sending plumes of dirt and grass scattering into the air. Within seconds, the plumes began reforming, coalescing and swirling to form something new above the crater.

I blinked.

The crater was gone. A lovely pebble path lined by daffodils and tulips took the place of the crater. The path led to the swirling dirt and grass as it solidified into something thin but sturdy. I couldn't tell what the object was yet.

Four hundred feet.

Things were different now, but that didn't stop my heart from thumping loudly. The wind sheared through my hair. My fingers were numb from the cold.

Two hundred feet.

Something was happening. The wind had swelled, and I could feel its intense focus on me.

One hundred feet.

The air condensed until it was nearly saturated. I could feel it coiling around me, latching onto my arms, my torso, my legs.

Fifty feet.

The wind shot its tendrils in every direction, like a spider web of particulate matter and water vapor, yet impossibly stronger. The air tugged me into its web, and beads of supersaturated moisture dripped onto my skin as the wind tucked around me tighter and tighter, forming a dangerous cocoon.

My feet suddenly touched something hard, and the wind evaporated into delicate whisps, melting the sunny day into a realm of sparkling fog. I stumbled as the wind relinquished the last of its support. My knee hit a patch of grass as I faltered.

"I'm alive," I whispered in surprise. I ran my hands through the blades of grass, soaking in the feeling of solid earth. Dew began to form on the tips of the blades under the thick fog. I sat up, giving my swimming head a moment to settle. The fog—the remnants of my reason for survival—blotted out the fluffy clouds and the innocent blue sky. Light still found a way through, but it was stunted and fragmented, sending the day into premature dusk.

The ground I sat on was relatively flat, indicating that I was likely either at the top or bottom of a hill. The heavy fog obscured everything in front of me, so I glanced over my shoulder, trying to get my bearings.

The tidy gravel path with its daffodils and tulips was there. I sucked in a breath, though I shouldn't have been surprised. However, I couldn't see the object at the end of the path that had been formed from the plume of dirt and grass. I'd have to go down the path to find out what it was.

I shook my head and sighed. Of course I would.

"Fine," I muttered as I stood and wiped the dewy moisture from the grass on my pants. "Beats falling through the sky again."

The pebbles crunched under my shoes as I walked. The path meandered more than I'd expected, and it was taking disconcertingly long to reach the end. Minutes ticked by. The fog dissipated into mist, but I still couldn't see the end.

The path hadn't seemed this long from above.

Crunch. Crunch. Crunch.

I shoved my worry down. Something would happen, eventually.

It always did.

So I kept walking, waiting for something to happen to me, to push me forward into the next stage. An hour passed with nothing to show for it.

My lips pinched together, and I paused, my shoe disrupting a pink tulip that had sprouted up just inside the edge of the path.

"Hey, watch it!" the pink tulip barked, its voice high and tiny.

My eyes bulged, and I quickly moved my shoe away.

"I-I'm sorry!" I blurted. "I didn't see you there!"

"Clearly," the pink tulip snipped. It made a show of glancing down at its stem and huffing. "Look here. You've scuffed me! And I wanted to make show this season." The flower pouted.

I dropped to a knee. "I'm truly sorry about that.

Really! But . . . you'll grow back next season, right?"

The tulip waved a delicate green leaf. "Yes, I'm a garden tulip, *obviously*, and it gets plenty cold here. Of course I'll grow back, but it won't be until next season! Do you know what it's like to have to wait *an entire year* for something? It's exhausting! I already put in so much effort this year! And you ruined it in two seconds."

I had the mind to look abashed, at least. "I'm very sorry. I didn't mean to! There's all this mist about, and I've been walking forever . . . plus, you're growing a bit further in than the others, you know."

The tulip snorted. "Oh, so it's *my* fault, is it? Do you want me to apologize for *your* lack of observation skills? Is that it?"

I waved my hands. "No, no, of course not! I was simply pointing out that anyone could have stepped on you in these conditions."

"And *that* makes it okay?"

"Well, no . . ."

"So what do you want from me?"

"I only meant to apologize."

"Then I don't accept your apology."

I blinked. What was I supposed to do now?

"Mysterious path got your tongue?"

I blinked again. "What?"

The pink tulip tsked. "If you can't even handle me, you're gonna have a riot on your hands in *there*."

"In where?"

The tulip tilted its petals toward the front of the path. "Through that door, of course. My, you are dense, aren't you?"

I scrunched my lips together as I followed the tulip's direction. A brown wooden door stood fortified amongst the mist, not three feet away from us. The door was made of a brilliant old wood, sturdy and stained with a clear lacquer that brought out its magnificent grains. It was framed in by matching brown beams, and layers of trim added a simple antique elegance to the structure. It looked like something out of a grand hall from the seventeenth century.

"How did that get there?" I asked the tulip, even though I didn't expect a straight answer.

The tulip tsked again. "You pay the fee, you get to go through the door. What else is there to it?" The flower eyed me shrewdly. "You *did* pay the fee, right? I don't know how you'd get this far if you hadn't, but every now and then someone tries."

"What's the fee?"

"So you didn't pay it," the tulip said flatly.

"I didn't say that! I just . . . want to make sure I paid the correct fee. That's all."

"Uh-huh. How about you tell me what you did pay, and I'll say if it is correct."

"Uhh . . ." I thought back to the fog and its cocoon and to falling through the sky and to nearly hitting the ground but finding out it was made of paper and to dumbly throwing gems at the ground. "Oh! Um, I paid one emerald and one ruby?"

The tulip gave me a doubtful look. "*You* paid that? Are you sure?"

I glanced over myself. "What? Should I have done something else?"

The tulip shook its petals. "No, that's fine, actually. I'm just a little surprised."

"So I'm good on the fee?"

"Yes."

I shoved my hands in my empty pockets. "Okay, then. I'll just go through the door now?"

"That's what it's there for, yes."

"Goodbye then, I suppose." I stood and took a step forward before glancing back at the pink tulip. "Oh, and sorry again about your stem. I hope you do well next year!"

"Just leave already," the tulip retorted.

"Yep, I'm going."

I approached the door and reached for the carved bronze handle. A zap of electricity tickled my fingers as I turned the handle. The elegant door creaked open, and ochre sunlight fell across my face. My chest swelled with an overwhelming surge of pride and hope, and a gleaming smile broke out across my face. I could once again see the undulating green hills before me, the baby blue sky and cotton ball clouds untouched. Dreams of success and achievement filled my mind, and anything seemed possible.

My hand was still braced against the bronze door knob, and I glanced over my shoulder at the path behind me. The mist and dim light twisted around the pebbles and flowers, a despairing sight compared the hope and sunshine atop the grassy hills.

It was an easy choice. My hand slid off the handle, and the door began to creak closed.

The tulip's voice suddenly squeaked out, "Don't forget to—"

The heavy door slammed shut.

CHAPTER TEN

PAPER TAPESTRIES: PART B

"Oops," I muttered. Then I shook my head. "It probably doesn't matter. The tulip just wanted to send my off with another snippy response. Nothing important."

I gazed over the rolling hills, filled with excitement. In the far-off distance, faints whisps began to sparkle and glow, and I knew, *just knew*, that my Hopes and Dreams were over there. I had to reach them! The hills would be a little cumbersome to traverse, but I didn't think it would take that long to reach the hill in the distance, the hill that sparkled and glowed with promises.

I lifted my leg, about to take my first step, when

suddenly a wall popped up in front of me. I skirted backwards in shock.

"What now?" I whined.

The wall was made of gray cinderblock and coated in a steel-blue layer of thick paint. It rose about ten feet higher and was just as long. I cautiously ran my hand along its surface, waiting to see if something terrible happened. A few flecks of paints fell off, but that was it.

I cocked my head, surveying the wall. A few of the cinderblocks were starting to crumble, but the paint held them together well enough. There was no door, no windows, no posters or paintings adorning its face. I slid back another step.

I could easily go around it. There's nothing here to stop me.

I slowly walked around the corner, keeping my eyes glued to the wall's peeling surface. Was this a trap, or was this what I was supposed to do?

As soon as a passed the wall, I glanced back, wanting to make sure that the wall hadn't suddenly shifted into a monster with razor sharp teeth.

The pro: the wall hadn't become a monster. The con:

the wall had disappeared altogether.

Fueled by inertia, my body kept walking despite my head angled over my shoulder and my mouth hanging open. Then an external force in the form of a hulking cinderblock wall interacted with my body, bringing me to a full stop as I slammed into it. I gasped and backed up, rubbing my sore nose.

"What? How?" The same cinderblock block wall now loomed before me. My head swiveled back and forth, double checking that the wall behind me had somehow jumped in front.

Anger bubbled up inside me, fueled by stubbornness. "Fine," I spat. "I don't have to walk forward. I'll simply pick another direction."

I marched to my left, thoroughly ignoring the cinderblock wall.

However, the wall turned out to be rather relentless. I'd made it three steps at most before the wall appeared in front of me again, stretching out like it wasn't a hunk of sentient cement and pigments. To my right, the sparkling whisps around the glowing hill remained far off in the distance. I slowly angled my body back toward my Hopes and Dreams. The cinderblock wall appeared in front of me again.

My shoulders fell in disappointment. "I have to deal with you, don't I?"

The wall didn't respond.

I groaned, rubbing my face. "Why does it always have to be difficult?" I complained. "Why can't I have a goal and reach it with ease?"

The wall remained silent.

"Fine, keep your secrets. I'll figure this out on my own."

I paced back and forth by the wall, trying to figure out the puzzle. I eyed the crumbly bits of cinderblock and the peeling paint.

"All I need to do is get past you, right?" I ran my fingers along a corner of brick that looked ready to break away. Dust and paint flecks came off in my hand. I pried at it, and more came away easily. I scuffed my shoe against another brick near the ground, fragments of cinderblock breaking away until there was a divot just big enough for the front of my shoe to fit inside. I gazed at the top of the wall.

Ten feet's not that high. I can do it.

And so I began to climb, prying away crumbling gray cinderblock as I went. I slipped once and scraped my knee on the side of the wall. My hands were covered in cement dust and indentations by the time I reached the top. I sat with my legs dangling over the edge, catching my breath. The wall hadn't disappeared, so I assumed I made the correct choice. I stared off into the distance, watching my Hopes and Dreams shimmer and sparkle.

They're so far away.

I worried about the distance between me and them. That was a lot of space for more walls to pop up.

Will I need to climb every one of them?

My fingers and knees would be bloody stumps by the end.

The space station wouldn't do that to me . . . would it?

I shook my head, not wanting to dwell on those thoughts. Besides, I wouldn't get to my Hopes and Dreams by sitting here. I peeked over the edge of the wall. Would it hurt if I jumped from ten feet?

My vision swam with vertigo, and I swallowed the nausea forming in my gut. Somehow, falling through the air hundreds of feet up was easier than jumping from ten feet off the ground. I turned around, letting my legs slide over the edge while my hands clutched the top of the wall. I kicked at the cinderblocks, trying to feel for footholds.

Going up is easier than going down.

A section gave way, and I jammed my foot inside. I lowered myself down, kicking at the cinderblock until another foothold fell out. My fingertips were just barely holding onto the top of the wall.

Now for the hard part—finding a handhold.

I carefully released one hand from the wall and probed around the surface of the cinderblocks for loose cement. One section crumbled under my touch, but I had to reach to get to it. I stretched my arm.

I have to let go of the wall.

My fingers were already slipping. I let them fall, pushing my weight into my feet and using my other hand to balance myself. When I remained attached to the wall, I let out a small "whoop!" of delight.

Of course, that was when a patch of cinderblock under my left foot crumbled entirely. I faltered as my foot slipped, but my grip wasn't strong enough, and I fell backwards off the wall.

I hit the ground hard then rolled; the short grass was not an excellent cushion, and I was on top of a hill. I blundered down the mild incline until the trifle of a valley lulled my speed. I laid there, sprawled on my face, grass and dirt in my mouth and hair and smeared on my shirt and pants, as I reconsidered my life choices.

After several minutes, I forced myself to sit up. The wall remained behind me, and I smiled.

I pushed myself up and trudged up the next hill. Once there, I gazed out over the landscape until my eyes found the sparkling air and glimmering hill. I sighed with contentment.

"That wasn't so bad," I said now that I was no longer dangling from atop the cinderblock wall. I placed my hands on my hips and confidently stepped forward.

A new cinderblock wall appeared. My smile faltered.

A breeze caused the new wall to flutter, the sound of snapping paper emanating from it. I titled my head in confusion. Then I walked forward and poked the wall. It bent around my finger like a moist towel. I pushed a little harder until the wall tore and my hand plunged through the gap. I screamed and pulled my hand back, suddenly worried I'd shoved it into an alternate dimension where organic life couldn't survive. I surveyed my hand, but it looked no different than usual.

I bent down, staring at the space beyond the hole. Rolling green hills and blue sky greeted me. I chuckled nervously.

"I'm being silly. Why would I think something would go wrong?"

Knowing I'd have to pass through—or over—this wall too, I grasped the edges of the hole and pulled, tearing the wall until there was a big enough opening for me to walk through. I made it to the other side of the wall without problem. I glanced back, happy to see both the wet towel wall and the crumbling wall both standing behind me.

Hill after hill stood between me and my Hopes and Dreams, and I was beginning to think that each one would carry a wall I'd have to surpass. Doubt niggled at me, but I carried on.

The next hill's wall had groups of shapes attached to it. The shapes were solid and empty circles, squares, and triangles, and there were five clusters of the shapes arranged in different sequences. An empty space on the wall and a smattering of the shapes on the ground told me that I needed to complete the sequence. I studied the existing clusters for nearly a minute before I noticed the pattern. I grabbed a solid triangle, empty circle, solid circle, and solid square from the ground and arranged them on the wall. As soon as I'd placed the last shape, the wall split apart down the middle, and I walked through.

There were now three walls behind me.

The next hill's wall appeared as a pile of rubble. I attempted to simply walk over it, but the rubble pile materialized in front of me again. After rolling my eyes, I noticed a bucket of lumpy gray sludge off to the side with a mortar trowel leaning against it.

I pinched my lips together and muttered, "I'm not sure how *building* a wall will help me get through it." Nonetheless, I bent down and organized my first row of bricks, slathering a layer of mortar on top and adding a second layer. I repeated this until I couldn't reach any higher. Luckily, that was also when the rubble pile ran out of bricks. I waited for the wall to move or break or do *something*, but it stood still as a mountain.

"Great. Just great!" I went to lean against the wall as I

waited for the structure to move, but my back didn't find solid matter. I stumbled backward, righting myself as the world distorted around me like a fishbowl. I sucked in a breath then wished I hadn't; the air tasted metallic and syrupy.

"What the—?" My voice came out wrong, croaky and unnaturally deep.

I waved my hand back and forth, but it took some effort, like I was moving through a thick pudding. I stepped forward, and my head popped back into normal reality. I quickly pulled the rest of myself out of the distortion.

When I noticed three walls on the hills in front of me, and I groaned, realizing I'd come out the wrong side. I peered behind me, noting that the wall I'd constructed remained there, waiting for me to walk through it. I sighed then stepped back inside, holding my breath this time. The world warped and slid against my skin as I plowed through. A whole minute passed before I emerged out the other side. I surveyed the landscape behind me, counting.

Four walls.

I nodded to myself before climbing up the next hill.

The wall that appeared when I reached the top of the hill felt different, which was saying something. Colorful light caught between the bricks, gyrating in a strange but oddly familiar manner. I peered at the light, leaning in close enough to stick out my finger and prod the bricks.

As soon as my finger got within an inch of the colorful light, it froze. I sucked in a breath, nervous. The light seemed to hover between the bricks, like it was waiting for me.

"What are you?" I whispered.

The light pulsed once.

It can hear me. No. It can understand *me.*

"Why—why do you look so familiar?"

In the center of the wall, the colorful light began to drip out of the space between the bricks. The light pulsed with the extra illumination from the sun above, almost like it was absorbing energy directly from the star.

The light dripped over several bricks until it began to form strange shapes that wiggled in ways I'd seen before.

A cold sweat covered me.

"No," I whispered. Then louder, "No. No, I can't do this!"

The wiggling light transported me back to a room where everyone else knew what was happening except me. A place where the strange dark shadow creatures communicated in odd tones and garbled sounds, and where the written language was too bizarre and celestial for me to comprehend.

"I didn't understand you before," I told the light. "I still haven't learned, so how am I supposed to solve this one?"

Panic began to twist around my gut. If I couldn't figure out this puzzle, then my journey was over. I would never reach the glimmering hill that sparkled with promises.

The light pulsed again. I stared at it with anxiety and frustration.

"*You* can understand *me*, apparently. So let me spell it out for you: I. Don't. Understand!"

The light paused then, almost gently, pulsed three times, yet each pulse was . . . different than the others. I frowned, trying to figure out how. The light had looked the same and the interval between pulses had been the same. So what was it?

The light pulsed three times again, and again I had the same feeling that each pulse was different.

"I," I said on a whim.

The colorful light swirled—almost like a smile—before pulsing once. *Pulse one.*

"Don't."

The light replicated the second pulse in its sequence. *Pulse B.*

"Understand." I held my breath.

The light pulsed in response. *Pulse X.*

I took a chance and said, "Hello."

The light responded. *Pulse five hundred and eighty-two.*

I backed up a step, trying to comprehend this nonlinear language that somehow linked to senses I'd never felt before. It wasn't like telepathy or dreams, or touch, smell, sound, sight, or taste. It was an entirely new sensation, like discovering I'd had an extra hand I'd forgotten about for my entire life.

The light and I continued to talk, trading words and vocabulary, then sentence structure, and finally complex ideas and nuances. Time held no meaning—it never did in the space station—as the light and I finally, *finally*, came to an intimate understanding.

I knew how to read the wiggling light, and I knew that I would be able to understand the shadow creatures if our paths ever crossed again.

A tidal wave of confidence hit me, and I suddenly knew what it felt like to succeed, to excel at something, to truly *know* something.

The colorful light pulsed in what I knew was pleasure and celebration. Then, more of the light between the bricks began to seep out from the crevices, covering the entire wall in shapes that no longer looked strange to me. I easily translated the writings on the wall, speaking the words aloud in both my own language and the gargled tones of the shadow creatures.

As the last syllable of the last word left my tongue, the wall dissolved into spurts of light frozen in place. The colorful light spun around the frozen light, almost like a miniature alien rave. The light told me it was having fun. It asked if I wanted to join.

I almost said yes, but as I peered through the wall of dissolved light, I couldn't help but stare at the outline of the many hills to go before I reached my true destination.

"I should go," I said to the light, my tone reluctant. The light pulsed in understanding and told me I could come back at any time, and that they always had room for one more person.

The light's words gave me pause, though I didn't know why, and I felt a little better about my decision to move on. If I went with the light, would I ever be able to come back to myself?

I walked through the wall of dissolved light, and as the streams of colorful light brushed against my skin, I could have sworn I heard the voices of people speaking in my native language. The voices swam together in hushed cacophony, and I couldn't distinguish any distinct words. The tones chilled me. Some were joyous and ecstatic, but others carried tears and regrets.

I was happy when I cleared the wall of light and continued to the next hill.

Five walls.

On and on it went, hours of climbing hills and puzzling through wall after wall. I paused on a hill to catch my breath, noting that I'd barely made it halfway.

"Come on!" I shouted at the undulating landscape. "Am I really supposed to keep grinding through task after task until I eventually make it to the end?" I didn't see the point in that, even if I eventually made to the glimmering hill that promised everything I wanted.

That realization made me pause—if all my Hopes and Dreams weren't worth the effort required to get to them, then where did that leave me?

I sat down on the hill, my heavy thoughts weighing on me. The air sparkled around the hill in the distance. The physical embodiment of all my Hopes and Dreams. But I had to ask myself—were those still *my* Hopes and Dreams?

The last hour, and all the distorted time before that, had been filled with countless physical and mental tasks, and I was beginning to wonder what the point of it all was. I couldn't see the connections between everything. I didn't know if there were any to begin with. What if there was no meaning in what I'd been doing, no meaning to any of it?

Despair, the feeling familiar to me by now, pricked my toes and began pooling in my feet. As my thoughts continued to spiral, the despair seeped higher and higher, filling my legs, then my stomach before crushing my lungs. I knew I shouldn't let it reach my heart. I *knew* it.

But I felt helpless to stop it.

And what was the point of stopping it, if there was no point to any of this at all?

Something bit my finger—it was no more than a sharp pinch—but it startled me, and I snatched my hand from the ground and held it to my chest, shouting, "Ouch!" more out of shock than pain. A tiny green body slithered away and into a hole before I could properly berate the creature.

"Rude," I said, pouting. I'd been in a proper moment of despair, and it had ruined it. Though, not entirely. The despair was still there. I could feel it waiting just below my heart, waiting for the moment I told it to continue. To consume me.

Twin droplets of blood welled on my finger. I gazed at them, suddenly aware that there were two of them. At least they had each other.

I held my hand close as I watched the lovely landscape of hills and walls. The sky was still blue, the clouds still made of cotton balls, and the sun never set in a place like this.

I'd done every task by myself. The closest thing to company I've had were woodland creatures, creepy Perfects, and sentient light.

Loneliness began to displace the despair, though not by much. Both feelings now threatened to drown me instead of just the one.

"I'd like someone to talk to," I said. I was surprised I'd spoken out loud. It shouldn't make any difference, but it felt momentous to me, like I was finally confessing what I really wanted out of life.

The clouds stopped moving.

"I want people—someone who will challenge my thoughts and will tell me things I've never heard before."

I also wanted someone who could hug me like the trees never could, but I wasn't ready to voice those thoughts just yet. One step at a time.

The sky shifted from blue to teal.

One step at a time.

One step at a time.

I sighed. Was life always just one step at a time? Would it ever be anything more, or anything less?

The walls behind me stood like trophies on a shelf, sturdy reminders of everything I'd accomplished. I should be proud, but an errant thought that I hadn't needed to complete these tasks alone poked at my mind.

"I . . . Can I ask for help?" Was I allowed to do that? Would something bad happen if I did?

The sun bubbled with red energy, steadily expanding as it burst with a new purpose.

"I'd like help. And a friend."

The sun continued expanding until it covered the entire sky in crimson hues, its death nearly complete. The green grass fizzled in the new light, some patches turning brown and decaying within seconds, others catching fire and burning to charred crisps almost instantaneously.

All around me the picturesque landscape of blue sky and lolling green hills was being replaced by an apocalypse.

I did this. I wanted to change things. I wanted to question how things were done, how life was meant to be lived, and, in the process, I'd done exactly what I wanted to: I destroyed my world.

New things didn't have to come from destruction, but they often did when radical change was involved.

Meteorites illuminated the bleeding sky like sparks of lightning in a cosmic storm. Chunks of rock and metal struck the hills, each impact another lash of drums marching to war. Electricity sparked between my toes and danced across the hair on my skin. Heat washed over me in toxic waves, yet I didn't feel like I was burning.

Hills were demolished faster than I could blink, yet the completed walls behind me were left unscathed. A few hills bravely fought back against the meteorites and the red giant. For their courage, they were allowed to remain. The others were reduced to embers in winding paths between the survivors. These new paths fanned out in all directions, leading to unknown destinations.

My glimmering hill with air that sparkled and shimmered around it . . . was gone.

All my Hopes and Dreams no longer rested in one place.

A place I'd not truly wanted anyway.

As the universe I existed in continued to destroy itself on my command, I smiled and picked a path that looked promising. After walking on it for perhaps a minute or maybe a century, a tall metal door suddenly appeared and *whooshed* open.

A red light shone through the open metal door.

Whatever I'd done had changed things everywhere.

I stepped through the door after only a moment of hesitation.

CHAPTER ELEVEN

THE FINAL SPHERE

The room was dark. There were no windows to the outside, at least that I could see. The edges of the sphere disappeared into the shadows. There were no distant stars or exploded nebulas to greet me.

I could hear a faint *beep beep beep* in the distance, a muted sound originating far beyond my current sphere. There was a sharp *CLANK*, and another metallic shell closed around my sphere, cutting off the sound of the alarm completely.

There was only silence.

A light flickered on in the center of the sphere, illuminating a single baren bench.

I shifted, the small scuff of my shoe on the metal floor deafening in the dark space. I waited, observing the solemn bench.

Is this the end?

Nothing happened. I remembered my lessons from the previous spheres: I could be the catalyst; I could change things, but I had to be willing to do it.

I sat on the bench, facing the expanse of darkness in front of me.

More lights flickered on, their light more gray than yellow, revealing a blank metal wall. I waited, but again nothing more happened.

I was willing to change things, but tendrils of doubt poked at me.

Can I change anything, or are there limits? How much of my life is within my control?

Control could only be an illusion, and I might never know. The thought unsettled me, but a part of me pushed back against the despair and panic. Giving up did nothing. Absolutely nothing. Even if I couldn't control everything, I could still try, and perhaps that was the meaning of existence. Simply doing. I could choose where I went and the meanings of the actions I chose.

I have more control than I thought. I can decide my

purpose and how I accomplish it, or even if I have more than one purpose.

I stared at the blank wall, resolve and contentment slowing displacing the despair and panic that had threatened to consume me not long ago.

"Show me what I'm supposed to see," I commanded the sphere.

Small windows, no bigger than a square foot each, opened across the empty wall. Every sphere I'd been in since entering the space station was visible through these windows. I saw the waiting room, the grasshoppers that liked to hear my stories, the shadow creatures with their tacky posters, the crossroads, the maze of other lands, the exploded nebula, the talking wrens, the Perfects and their Mirrors, and, finally, the burning landscape that had once held hills of green.

This room was not a window on the wall.

I studied each of the spheres, each version of reality and experiences I'd gone through, and waves of emotions hit me. Joy. Discomfort. Confusion. Curiosity. Fear. Resolve. Confidence. Doubt. Despair. Contentment. Determination.

The length of time I'd been in the space station was innumerable by my perception, but it had captured my life thus far in its entirety. Different scenes, same feelings. Same landscapes, new perspectives.

My whole life, reduced to a handful of windows on a wall.

So . . . this is the end, then? All I am, all I chose to be, is here?

The thought didn't sit quite right with me. It felt wrong. Incomplete. Why allow change and growth if this was it? I decided that there *must* be more, if for nothing other than the opportunity to experience life with the changes I'd made to myself.

Life shouldn't stop just when it's getting started.

I felt as heavy as the core of Jupiter from my thoughts, yet my body lifted off the bench like I was on a meager asteroid. I was standing, and my hands clenched of their own accord. Knowing the importance of what I was doing, I turned, ever so slowly, to see the rest of the room.

I gasped, despite knowing it would be different this time.

Lights illuminated the walls, and each surface—the

ceiling and floor included—displayed countless windows. I frowned at the sight before me. Each window was tinted a dark gray, obscuring whatever was behind it.

This last sphere—it was merely another crossroads along my journey, a journey with more possibilities than I'd foreseen.

"Show me all the worlds with friends," I commanded.

Dozens and dozens of windows lit up, colorful and bleak worlds alike displayed behind them. Dozens more windows remained gray and lifeless.

"Show me the worlds with love."

Several of the illuminated windows went dark while a dozen more sprung to life. I was pleased that many of the already lit worlds remained on.

"Show me the worlds that will inspire me."

More windows lit up while some darkened.

And so I asked the sphere question after question, watching the windows die and spring to life. I didn't pay attention to each world; I didn't want to know the future, only that the possibilities I desired existed. Dozens and dozens of worlds remained lit despite my barrage of questions, and I felt myself tear up with a new kind of happiness I'd never felt before. It was part elation, part contentment, part relief, and part excitement.

After my mind had been exhausted of all my questions, I closed my eyes, bathing in this feeling, in my new knowledge of life.

Seconds, or maybe eons, passed before I opened my eyes again. The walls were once more empty and shrouded in edgeless shadows. Only a single metal door stood before me on the far wall. It *whooshed* open with a flowery breeze that reminded me of dogwood blossoms. Delicate light filtered through the open door, clinging to the frame like jelly and amalgamating with the darkness in the room like oil mixing with water.

I smiled, ready for the new life that awaited me.

As I stepped through the door, the space station allowed me to catch a glimpse of reality outside. Two black holes collided and merged into a singular, supermassive black hole. Five stars nearby went supernova, flinging rings of gorgeous gas out into the universe in colorful waves, their neutrons cores burning with condensed excitement. Galaxies rammed into each other, intertwining in parts and slowly wreaking havoc on the thousands of systems within their domains. Twelve thousand new stars were born in spasms of light and dust inside a nebula that spanned the width of an entire galaxy. Dust and ice accreted around the new stars, spinning and coalescing until rocky and gaseous planets and moons formed. Chunks of unused rock and metal crashed into some of the new planets and moons, reshaping and forming and sometimes killing them. Gaseous planets changed their orbits, each new solar system wobbly until equilibrium was reached. Comets collided with the rocky planets, delivering water and minerals. Plants and species developed, and civilizations were created, fell, and rose again.

Paradise grew from simple dust. From the destruction of the old came new life and new opportunities, yet everything was still made of the same base elements.

I was me, yet now I was *beyond* me.

THANKS FOR READING!

Hello, and thanks for reading Space Station! If you'd like to check out my writing progress, updates and new releases, and ongoing promotional events, please check out my website at www.krgadeken.com.

Customer reviews allow independent authors to continue sharing their stories. If you enjoyed this book, please leave a review on your chosen platform.

Thank you!

Acknowledgements

A heartfelt thanks to all my beta readers for always reading my drafts and providing helpful feedback.

A special thanks to the library crew for helping get this project started.

And, finally, a hearty thanks to John and our cat Malo for their unwavering support and constant encouragement.

ABOUT THE AUTHOR

K.R. Gadeken was born and raised in Northern Colorado, where she found a love for the mountain wilderness and exploration at an early age. She traveled around the world before returning to Colorado to earn a Bachelor's in Astronomy. She later moved to Tennessee with her partner and earned a Master's in Geography. As an author, she uses her career as an excuse to read far too many books. She is the author of the Nabukko Trilogy, and you can visit her online at krgadeken dot com and on social media.

THE NABUKKO
TRILOGY

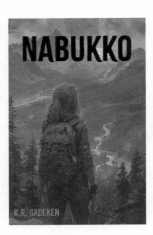

Eff wakes up on a strange planet, her memories fractured and missing. After months of solitary exploration, a chance encounter with a group of colonists changes everything, catapulting Eff into far more mysteries, secrets, and bizarre circumstances than she could have ever bargained for. Can she trust these colonists? Why does she get the feeling they are hiding something? And how is she tied to their mysterious circumstances? Captivating, suspenseful, cerebral, and filled with mystery, *Nabukko* is the first book in a young adult science fiction trilogy.

Praise for the Nabukko Trilogy

"Gadeken has delivered a unique, richly woven story brimming with intrigue and mystery ... *Nabukko* is a remarkable, multi-layered science fiction novel with endearing characters, perplexing mysteries, and unforgettable scenes." —*BlueInk, starred review*

"Boasting a nebulous puzzle of a plot, this novel is paced to perfection, with character and story revelations happening on a slow drip that makes it hard to stop reading." —*Self-Publishing Review*

"Superlative characters and worldbuilding ensure this SF tale will linger for some time." —*Kirkus Reviews*